DINOSAURS
— FROM —
HEAD TO TAIL

WRITTEN BY **Stacey Roderick**

ILLUSTRATED BY **Kwanchai Moriya**

Kids Can Press

What dinosaur had
a head like this?

A Parasaurolophus!

With a long, curved crest on its head, the Parasaurolophus (PAIR-ah-SORE-all-uh-FUS) might have been the kind of dinosaur that liked to toot its own horn! Some scientists think these dinos communicated with one another by pushing air through the hollow tubes in their crests to make low noises that sounded something like foghorns.

What dinosaur had jaws like this?

A Tyrannosaurus!

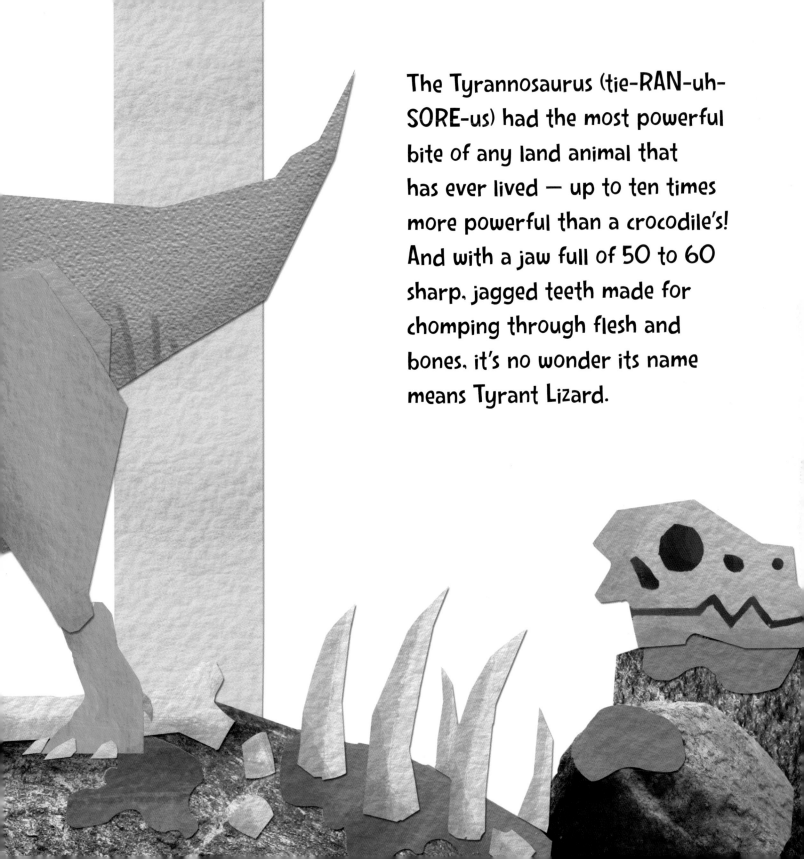

The Tyrannosaurus (tie-RAN-uh-SORE-us) had the most powerful bite of any land animal that has ever lived — up to ten times more powerful than a crocodile's! And with a jaw full of 50 to 60 sharp, jagged teeth made for chomping through flesh and bones, it's no wonder its name means Tyrant Lizard.

What dinosaur had a neck like this?

A Diplodocus!

With a neck that stretched about 6 meters (20 feet), the Diplodocus (dih-PLOD-uh-kus) was one of the longest dinosaurs. Such a long neck would have been very difficult to lift up high, so the Diplodocus likely just ate low-lying plants and trees. But since it could move its neck from side to side, it covered a lot of ground while standing in just one spot.

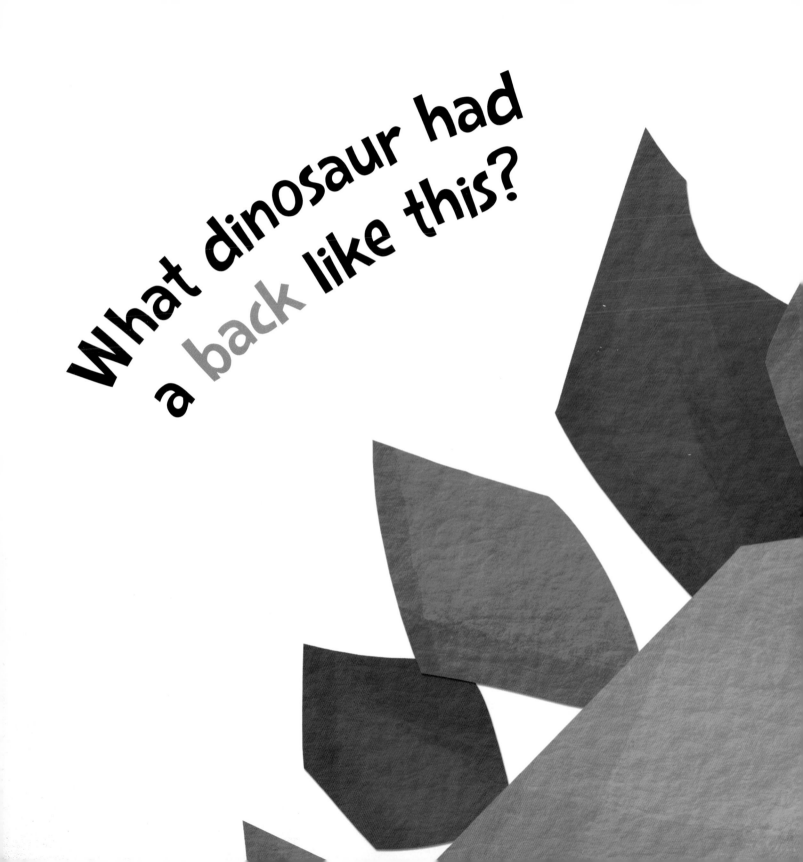

What dinosaur had a back like this?

A Stegosaurus!

The Stegosaurus (steg-uh-SORE-us) had two rows of sharp-edged plates running down its back. Scientists have a few ideas about why. The plates might have been a built-in heating and cooling system. If the dino needed to warm up, the plates soaked up heat from the sun. Or if it needed to cool down, the plates let off extra heat. The rows of plates might also have been a way for the Stegosauruses to recognize each other, as well as scare off any predators thinking about eating them.

What dinosaur had wings like this?

None!

These wings belong to the Pteranodon (teh-RAN-oh-don), which was not actually a dinosaur. But Pteranodons were close cousins of the dinosaurs and lived during the same time period. Pteranodons flew with wings made of thin skin that stretched from their long fourth fingers to the tops of their legs.

What dinosaur had claws like this?

A Therizinosaurus!

The Therizinosaurus (THER-uh-ZEEN-uh-SORE-us) had three giant claws on each of its front feet. The claws may have measured up to 1 meter (3 feet) — about as long as a baseball bat. No wonder this plant-eater's claws are thought to be the longest of any animal that has ever lived!

What dinosaur
had legs like this?

A Giganotosaurus!

The Giganotosaurus (gig-an-OH-toe-SORE-us) used its powerful, muscular legs to chase its prey. This massive meat-eater was what scientists call a biped, an animal that gets around using two legs. It was even bigger than another famous meat-eating biped — the Tyrannosaurus.

What dinosaur
had a tail like this?

An Ankylosaurus!

The Ankylosaurus (ank-EYE-low-SORE-us) probably used the rounded, bony ball on the end of its tail to protect itself from attacking predators. Scientists think that by swinging its tail from side to side like a club, it could have actually broken the bones of another dinosaur.

Other Awesome Dinosaurs

The Triceratops (tri-SARE-ah-tops) had three horns and a bony frill on its huge head.

The plant-eating Corythosaurus (core-ith-oh-SORE-us) had a beak-like mouth filled with hundreds of teeth for chewing.

Bony armor covered the Edmontonia (ED-mon-TONE-ee-ah), including large, ridged plates that protected its neck.

Meat-eating Spinosaurus (SPINE-oh-SORE-us) had a tall, spiny sail running down its back.

The Iguanodon (ig-WHA-noh-don) had a cone-shaped thumb spike on each hand.

The chicken-sized Compsognathus (komp-sog-NAY-thus) ran around on two skinny legs.

Like many large dinosaurs that walked on two feet, the Allosaurus (al-oh-SORE-us) had a thick, heavy tail that helped with balance.

For my Owenosaurus (OH-wen-oh-SORE-us) — S.R.
For Mommy and Papa — K.M.

Acknowledgments
Many thanks to David C. Evans, Ph.D., Curator of Vertebrate
Palaeontology, Department of Natural History (Palaeobiology), Royal
Ontario Museum, and to Donald Henderson, Ph.D., Curator
of Dinosaurs, Royal Tyrrell Museum, for generously sharing
their time and expertise to review this manuscript.

Kids Can Press acknowledges the financial support of
the Government of Ontario, through the Ontario Media
Development Corporation's Ontario Book Initiative; the
Ontario Arts Council; the Canada Council for the Arts;
and the Government of Canada, through the CBF, for
our publishing activity.

Published in Canada by
Kids Can Press Ltd.
25 Dockside Drive
Toronto, ON M5A 0B5

Published in the U.S. by
Kids Can Press Ltd.
2250 Military Road
Tonawanda, NY 14150

www.kidscanpress.com

The artwork in this book was created in Adobe Photoshop
and Illustrator, using original photographs and textures.

The text is set in Squidtoonz.

Edited by Stacey Roderick
Designed by Julia Naimska

This book is smyth sewn casebound.
Manufactured in Shenzhen, China, in 11/2014 by Imago

CM 15 0 9 8 7 6 5 4 3 2 1

Library and Archives Canada Cataloguing in Publication

Roderick, Stacey, author
    Dinosaurs from head to tail / written by Stacey
Roderick ; illustrated by Kwanchai Moriya.

ISBN 978-1-77138-044-7 (bound)

    1. Dinosaurs — Juvenile literature. I. Kwanchai, Moriya,
illustrator II. Title.

QE861.5.R63 2015   j567.9   C2014-902625-0

Kids Can Press is a ᶜorus™ Entertainment company